D1269489

This book belongs to the

Fabulous

The Fabulous Glitter Girl

Written by
Morgan Lee Scheel

Illustrated by
Angela Sbandelli

NEW YORK

NASHVILLE MELBOURNE

The Fabulous Glitter Girl

© 2017 Morgan Lee Scheel

Published in New York, New York, by Morgan James Publishing. Morgan James and The Entrepreneurial Publisher are trademarks of Morgan James, LLC. www.MorganJamesPublishing.com

Shelfie

A **free** eBook edition is available with the purchase of this print book.

ISBN 978-1-63047-998-5 paperback
ISBN 978-1-63047-999-2 eBook
ISBN 978-1-68350-000-1 casebound
Library of Congress Control Number: 2016904028

Cover Design by:
Angela Sbandelli

CLEARLY PRINT YOUR NAME ABOVE IN UPPER CASE
Instructions to claim your free eBook edition:
1. Download the Shelfie app for Android or iOS
2. Write your name in **UPPER CASE** above
3. Use the Shelfie app to submit a photo
4. Download your eBook to any device

with...
Habitat for Humanity®
Peninsula and Greater Williamsburg

In an effort to support local communities, raise awareness and funds, Morgan James Publishing donates a percentage of all book sales for the life of each book to Habitat for Humanity Peninsula and Greater Williamsburg.

Get involved today! Visit www.MorganJamesBuilds.com.

For Sophia Dorothea

You are my
whole wide world

Once upon a time,
in a
once upon a place,

There was a
once upon a story,
to put a smile
on your face!

There was a once upon a girl,
who lived in a once upon a world,
and her name was . . .

The Fabulous Glitter Girl!

She lived in the land of Glitter and Gleam
where everything sparkled
and happiness beamed.

The townspeople were friendly,
and kind as could be,
and everyone made sure to say
"thank you" and "please."

Bad things rarely ever happened
around Glitter town.

Bakery

Mr. Shine Bright

The crime rate was low,

and the King of the land was proud.

But every once in a while, some trouble would brew...

Like the day Fabulous Glitter Girl
hit the King on the head with a shoe.

Glitter Girl was fabulous, without any doubt,
but she had a few bad habits
she needed to work out.

She liked to play dress up and dance all day long.
She'd whirl and she'd twirl
to her favorite songs.

She did not like to listen when her mother would say
"Fabulous Glitter Girl, do your chores
before you run off and play."

Instead, she'd sneak off
to play dress up and dance,
avoiding her chores at each little chance.

Until one day . . .
The King of the land of Glitter and Gleam
was out taking a walk, enjoying the scene,

When out of the blue, a shoe
clunked him on the head.
It hit him so hard, everyone thought he was dead!

The townspeople quickly carried the king away,
back to the castle, calling the doctor on the way.

Dr. Gleamonowski came to see what she could do.
She first took an x-ray, then rubbed his head
with some GOO!

Her report was amazing,
could this really be true?
Was the king knocked unconscious
by Fabulous Glitter Girl's shoe?

The doctor reported to all the King's men
that the King would be fine after two days in bed.

Then, the town had a meeting to decide what to do.
They would have to investigate
Fabulous Glitter Girl and the shoe.

Tonight
shoe
investigation!

Detective Diamond was the first on the case.
"I will find out what happened, make no mistake!"

The very first thing he decided to do was to visit Fabulous Glitter Girl's house and investigate the shoe!

Fabulous Glitter Girl's mother exclaimed
"Oh my gosh, Oh my, my!"
Her father was angry
and let out a big sigh.

"That is my shoe, detective!"
Mrs. Glitter exclaimed,
when he showed them the shoe
with Fabulous Glitter Girl's name.

Mr. Glitter called Fabulous Glitter Girl
to come down from her room.

"Detective Diamond has a question
he'd like to ask you."
"Can you tell me why your name
is written on the bottom
of your mom's brand new shoes?"
Fabulous Glitter Girl began to cry
as she told him the truth.

Well, it turns out...

On that day Fabulous Glitter Girl
was supposed to be cleaning her room,
she had to organize her closet
and get her carpet vacuumed.

Instead, she'd been playing dress up
with her mom's brand new shoes,
and had been twirling and whirling
around in her room.

When all of a sudden, she heard her mom say
"I'm going to come check your room, then you can go play."

Fabulous Glitter Girl panicked and said "What will I do?"
"I'll get in trouble if mom finds me wearing her shoes!"

So... She ran to the window and opened it fast.
Around and around, Fabulous Glitter Girl dashed.

In the nick of time, she got the shoes off,
then wrote her name on the bottom,
just in case they got lost.

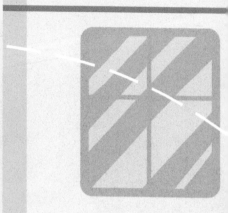

"I'll sneak out later to get them
when no one is there."
And she tossed the shoes into the air!
And that's when...
The King of the land of Glitter and Gleam
was out taking a walk, enjoying the scene.

He stopped to talk with the baker,
Mr. Shine Bright, just when
Fabulous Glitter Girl's shoes took flight!

"Looks like this case is solved, Detective Diamond!"
Mrs. Glitter exclaimed. "
And I do believe my daughter
has learned an important lesson today."

Please inform the King
"we will come to the castle at three,
so The Fabulous Glitter Girl
can apologize to thee!"

Fabulous Glitter Girl cried all the way into town.
It made her sad to see her parents'
smiles turned upside down.

And though she felt scared to apologize
to the town and the King,
she knew that telling the truth would be the very best thing.

"I learned that sneaking and lying is not very smart
and no matter what, you will always get caught!

I should not touch things that do not belong to me,
and I know now my actions can affect everyone, not just me!"

The town of Glitter and Gleam all cheered!
Then the King proclaimed
"All of us shall remember
this important lesson we learned today!"

That night, when Mrs. Glitter tucked
Fabulous Glitter Girl into bed,
she told her she was proud of her,
kissed her forehead and said,
"The reward is always bigger
when you tell the truth."

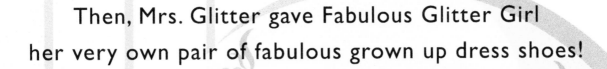

Then, Mrs. Glitter gave Fabulous Glitter Girl
her very own pair of fabulous grown up dress shoes!

The End

The Fabulous

HONEST PROMISE

I promise to do my best to tell the truth.
I will have the sparkle and courage to admit when I am wrong.
I understand that I am not always perfect, but I am always
FABULOUS!

Encourage your child to take the
Honest Promise Pledge with
The Fabulous Glitter Girl!

Visit us at www.fabulousglittergirl.com
to print out a colorful keepsake certificate for your child.

Morgan Lee Scheel, Author

Morgan Lee Scheel was born in Jersey City, New Jersey. As a child, she attended a private grammar school that focused on creative arts and had an advanced literature curriculum. Morgan loved to read. Late at night when the lights were shut off, she would hide under her covers and read with a flashlight or by the moonlight through her bedroom window. After completing a degree in liberal arts, she moved to Music City, USA, to pursue her love of writing and music in 2000.

Morgan has a real understanding of what children love because she loves the same things. She is the mother of a fabulous daughter and loves all things that are colorful, bright, happy, beautiful, and fun. Her motto in life is "Everything is better when you add some glitter!"

Angela Sbandelli, Illustrator

Italian illustrator Angela Sbandelli was born and currently resides in Siena, Italy. Angela graduated in 2004 from the 2D Animation program at the Academy of Digital Art Nemo and earned degree in communication science from the University of Florence in 2005. Angela has since worked on multiple animation projects, including the preschool television series *Pipi, Pupa and Rosemary*. Angela's work can be found in various children's books, as well as educational and activity books in Italy.

A free eBook edition is available with the purchase of this book.

To claim your free eBook edition:
1. Download the Shelfie app.
2. Write your name in upper case in the box.
3. Use the Shelfie app to **submit a photo**.
4. Download your **eBook to any device**.

Shelfie

A **free** eBook edition is available
with the purchase of this print book.

CLEARLY PRINT YOUR NAME ABOVE IN UPPER CASE

Instructions to claim your free eBook edition:
1. Download the Shelfie app for Android or iOS
2. Write your name in **UPPER CASE** above
3. Use the Shelfie app to submit a photo
4. Download your eBook to any device

Print & Digital Together Forever.

Snap a photo   Free eBook   Read anywhere

CPSIA information can be obtained
at www.ICGtesting.com
Printed in the USA
LVOW06*1417060217

523353LV00024B/421/P